Table of Contents

Winnie the Pooh

Deep in the Hundred Acre Wood
Where Christopher Robin plays
You'll find the enchanted neighborhood
Of Christopher's childhood days

A donkey named Eeyore is his friend
And Kanga and little Roo
There's Rabbit and Piglet and there's Owl
But most of all Winnie the Pooh

Chorus
Winnie the Pooh, Winnie the Pooh
Chubby little cubby all stuffed with fluff
He's Winnie the Pooh, Winnie the Pooh
Willy-nilly silly ole bear

Repeat chorus

3

Lyrics and music by Richard M. Sherman and Robert B. Sherman
© 1963 Wonderland Music Company, Inc. (BMI). Copyright renewed.

Introduction

Singing along, we come
Tigger, Rabbit, and I
To share this book with you.
Come join the fun and sing our songs
in the Hundred Acre Wood.

Come join the enchanted world of Pooh as you sing the twelve toe-tapping tunes that Pooh and his friends love to sing. There are silly songs—"The Wonderful Thing About Tiggers," mischievous songs— "Heffalumps and Woozles," birthday songs—"Pooh, Pooh, the Birthday Bear," rainy day songs—"The Rain, Rain, Rain Came Down, Down, Down," and marching songs—"Hip, Hip, Pooh-Ray." So clap your hands with Pooh. Stomp your feet with Pooh. You can even hippity-hop with Pooh. As you sing your way through the pages of this book and experience your own laughter and fun, you'll discover that it's just like the song says—"It's So Much More Friendly with Pooh."

Based on the "Winnie The Pooh" works ©A.A. Milne and E.H. Shepard.
© The Walt Disney Company
℗1995 Buena Vista Pictures Distribution, Inc.
Distributed by Walt Disney Records

Share the music of Disney at our website:
http://www.disney.com/records
ISBN: 1-55723-933-9

Burbank, CA 91521
Printed in U.S.A.

Walt Disney
RECORDS

Little Black Rain Cloud

I'm just a little black rain cloud
Hovering under the
honey tree
I'm only a little black
rain cloud
Pay no
attention to little me

Chorus
Oh, everyone knows
that a rain cloud
Never eats honey
no, not a nip
I'm just floating
around over the ground
Wondering where
I will drip

Repeat chorus

Lyrics and music by Richard M. Sherman and Robert B. Sherman
© 1963 Wonderland Music Company, Inc. (BMI). Copyright renewed.

4

It Really Was a Woozle,

Chorus

Well, it really was a woozle, yes it was, was, was
Why it really was a woozle, yes it was
Of course it was!
I'm sure because
I think I saw some woozle fuzz
It really was a woozle, yes it was

Once about a week ago
While walking in the wood
I saw some tracks around the trees
In Piglet's neighborhood
I said, "Hey, Piglet, look at that
Looks like a woozle paw!"
I'm telling you exactly what we saw

Repeat chorus

At first there was one
set of tracks
Then two, then three, then four
We walked around that tree again
And each time there were more

5

Lyrics by Mike Himelstein. Music by Steve Mayer.
© 1995 Walt Disney Music Company (ASCAP) /
Wonderland Music Company, Inc. (BMI)

Yes It Was

It absolutely positively
Left a woozle scent!
I wonder where in the world
the woozle went?

Repeat chorus

'Cause I know what a woozle does
And what a woozle doesn't
And if a woozle it was not

Then you are standing on the spot
Where a wise old woozle wasn't!
Well, we didn't exactly see one
But we knew it had to be one...

Repeat chorus
add: It was!

6

The Wonderful Thing About Tiggers

The wonderful thing about Tiggers
Is Tiggers are wonderful things
Their tops are made out of rubber
Their bottoms are made out of springs
They're bouncy, trouncy, flouncy, pouncy
Fun! Fun! Fun! Fun! Fun!
But the most wonderful thing about
Tiggers is
I'm the only one
I'm the only one

Repeat

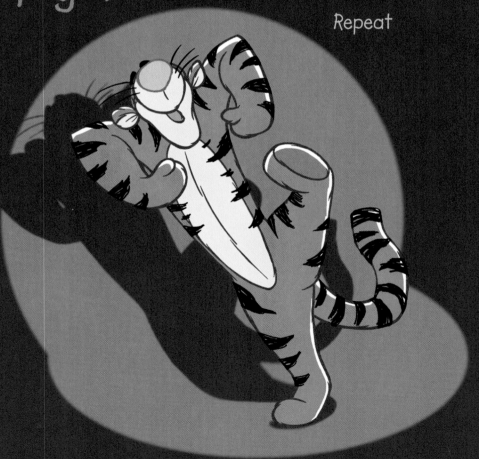

Lyrics and music by Richard M. Sherman and Robert B. Sherman
© 1964 Wonderland Music Company, Inc. (BMI). Copyright renewed.

Up, Down, and Touch the Ground

Up, down, up
When I up, down, touch the ground
It puts me in the mood
Up, down, touch the ground
In the mood for food

I am stout, round, and I have found
Speaking poundage wise
I improve my appetite
When I exercise

I am short, fat, and proud of that
And so with all my might
I up, down, and up and down
To my appetite's delight!

While I up, down, and touch
the ground
I think of things to chew
Like honey
With a hefty, happy appetite
I'm a hefty, happy Pooh

With a hefty, happy appetite
He's a hefty, happy Pooh

Lyrics and music by Richard M. Sherman and Robert B. Sherman
© 1963 Wonderland Music Company, Inc. (BMI). Copyright renewed.

Rumbly in My Tumbly

Hum da dee dum
Hum da dee dum
I'm so rumbly in my tumbly
Time to munch an early luncheon
Hum da dee dum dum

Oh, I wouldn't climb this tree
If a pooh flew like a bee
But I wouldn't be a bear then
So I guess I wouldn't care then!

Bears love honey and I'm a pooh bear
So I do care so I'll climb there
I'm so rumbly in my tumbly
Time for something sweet

Oh, I wouldn't climb this tree
If a pooh flew like a bee
But I wouldn't be a bear then
So I guess I wouldn't care then!

Bears love honey and
I'm a pooh bear
So I do care so I'll climb there
I'm so rumbly in my tumbly
Time for something sweet

10

Lyrics and music by Richard M. Sherman and Robert B. Sherman
© 1964 Wonderland Music Company, Inc. (BMI). Copyright renewed.

It's So Much More Friendly with Pooh

You can clap by yourself
You can snap by yourself
There's so many things
you can do
But it's so much more friendly
with Pooh

You can eat by yourself
Stomp your feet by yourself
There's so many things
you can do
But it's so much more friendly
with Pooh

I like to bounce with Tigger
With Kanga or Rabbit or Roo
With a friend
the fun gets bigger
'Cause there's so many things
that two can do

You can wiggle by yourself
You can giggle by yourself
There's a million things
you can do
But it's so much more friendly
with Pooh

You can hum by yourself
Play a drum by yourself
There's so many things
you can do
But it's so much more friendly
with Pooh

Now you're Piglet, and you're Pooh
Well, I'm me and you're you
If you count you and me that
makes two
'Cause it's so much
more friendly with
Much more friendly with
Much more friendly with Pooh

Lyrics by Mike Himelstein. Music by Terry Sampson.
© 1995 Walt Disney Music Company (ASCAP)

The Rain, Rain, Rain

Came

Down,

Down,

Down

The rain, rain, rain came down, down, down
in rushing rising riv'lets
Till the river crept out of its bed
and crept right into Piglet's!
Poor Piglet, he was frightened with
quite a rightful fright
And so in desperation a message he did write
He placed it in a bottle and it floated out of sight

And the rain, rain, rain came down, down, down
So Piglet started bailing
He was unaware, atop his chair
While bailing he was sailing
And the rain, rain, rain came down, down, down
And the flood rose up, up, upper
Pooh, too, was caught and so he thought
"I must rescue my supper"

Ten honey pots he rescued
Enough to see him through
But as he sopped up his supper
The river sopped up Pooh
And the water twirled and tossed him
in a honey pot

And the rain, rain, rain came down, down, down
So Piglet started bailing
He was unaware, atop his chair
While bailing he was sailing
And the rain, rain, rain came down, down, down
And the flood rose up, up, upper
Pooh, too, was caught and so he thought
"I must rescue my supper"

    Ten honey pots he rescued
    Enough to see him through
    But as he sopped up his supper
    The river sopped up Pooh
    And the water twirled and tossed him
    in a honey pot canoe

(The rain, rain, rain came down, down, down
When the rain, rain, rain came down, down, down)

Lyrics and music by Richard M. Sherman and Robert B. Sherman
© 1964 Wonderland Music Company, Inc. (BMI). Copyright renewed.

A Rather Blustery Day

Hum dum dum dee dee dum
Hum dum dum

Oh, the wind is lashing lustily
And the trees are thrashing thrustily
And the leaves are rustling gustily
So it's rather safe to say
That it seems that it may turn out to be
It feels that it will undoubtedly
Looks like a rather blustery day today
It seems that it may turn out to be
Feels that it will undoubtedly
Looks like a rather blustery day today

Lyrics and music by Richard M. Sherman and Robert B. Sherman
© 1964 Wonderland Music Company, Inc. (BMI). Copyright renewed.

Heffalumps and Woozles

They're black, they're brown, they're up, they're down
They're in, they're out, they're all about!
They're far, they're near, they're gone, they're here!
They're quick and slick, they're insincere!

Beware! Beware! Be a very wary bear

A heffalump or woozle is very confusil
A heffalump or woozle's very sly! (sly) (sly) (sly)
They come in ones and twosles but if they so choosles
Before your eyes you'll see them multiply (ply) (ply) (ply)

They're extraordinary so better be wary
Because they come in ev'ry shape and size (size) (size) (size)
If honey's what you covet, you'll find that they love it
Because they'll guzzle up the thing you prize

Beware! Beware! Be a very wary bear

(Instrumental chorus)

They're extraordinary so better be wary
Because they come in ev'ry shape and size (size) (size) (size)
If honey's what you covet, you'll find that they love it
Because they'll guzzle up the thing you prize

They're black, they're brown, they're up, they're down
They're in, they're out, they're all about!
They're far, they're near, they're gone, they're here!
They're quick and slick, they're insincere!

Beware! Beware! Beware!
Beware! Beware!

Lyrics and music by Richard M. Sherman and Robert B. Sherman
© 1964 Wonderland Music Company, Inc. (BMI). Copyright renewed.

Pooh, Pooh, the Birthday Bear

Ready, set, one, Pooh, Ee-yore
Sound the bells, go out and tell
The whole world that we're here
'Cause Pooh it's true we're throwing you
The grandest party of the year

Pooh, Pooh, the birthday bear
Today will be a Poohmongous affair
We've baked a homemade honey cake
And it looks so good we can't wait
So Pooh, please don't be late

All of us who have grown up
On Pooh philosophy
Now have gathered at the corner
To be part of history

Oh, Pooh, Pooh, the birthday bear
Today will be a Poohmongous affair
We've baked a homemade honey cake
And it looks so good we can't wait
So Pooh, please don't be late

Lyrics and music by Will Robinson
© 1995 Seven Summits Music (BMI)

I've never seen the woods so green
Or the sky so blue
I suppose that goes to show
There's no one quite like...

Pooh, Pooh, the birthday bear
Your friends are here to celebrate from everywhere
We've baked a homemade honey cake
And it looks so good we can't wait
Pooh, please don't be late
Pooh, you'd better not be late
Pooh, please don't be late

Hip, Hip, Pooh-Ray

We never will forget
Our hero of the wet
Our quick thinking
unsinking Pooh bear

Lyrics and music by Richard M. Sherman and Robert B. Sherman
© 1964 Wonderland Music Company, Inc. (BMI). Copyright renewed.

And Piglet who indeed
Helped out a friend in need
Truly they're the heroes of the day

So we say
Hip, hip, Pooh-ray
For the Piglet and the Pooh
Piglet and Pooh
We salute you

For deeds of bravery
And generosity
Hip, hip, Pooh-ray
Hip, hip, Pooh-ray
Hip, hip, Pooh-ray
For Winnie the Pooh
And Piglet, too

Walt Disney RECORDS

Burbank, CA 91521
Printed in U.S.A.